The Anchorman Murders

by

Ethel Headen

DORRANCE PUBLISHING CO., INC.
PITTSBURGH, PENNSYLVANIA 15222

This book is dedicated to one black man's struggle for equal employment in the late fifties, his achievements and rewards, only to be denied one of the greatest challenges of his career as an anchorman. It's about love, murder, trials, and tribulations.

I hope the many readers of this book who strive for an education in today's world will achieve their goals in life, because prejudice is going out slowly but surely.

This book is also dedicated to my granddaughter Yvone Toppin.

ISBN: 978-0-8059-7177-4

Printed in the United States of America

First Printing

For more information or to order additional books, please contact:
Dorrance Publishing Co., Inc.
701 Smithfield Street
Third Floor
Pittsburgh, Pennsylvania 15222
U.S.A.
1-800-788-7654
www.dorrancebookstore.com

Chapter One

It had been a long, hot summer and the coming of the fall was just around the corner. Most of us in the little country township of Cedar Grove were preparing our harvest for the winter months ahead. Our kids were looking forward to another school year. The older ones in their senior year were already talking about graduation.

One young man name John Brower had made it. He was the talk of Cedar Grove, North Carolina. The reason for all the talk was because John had been the first black from Cedar Grove ever to attend Howard University and graduate from their journalism school. John had been offered a job as a news anchor and writer in an northern city.

The oldest of seven children, his parents worked hard, priming tobacco to get their son through college. Nannie Mae, and old Willie Buck had the names that had been handed down through slavery. All of our names are Maes and Bucks, anyway; one would think they were celebrating the old days.

They prepared for John's arrival. Ella Mae, John's younger sister, was talking about the speech John was to make in church on Sunday. I could hardly wait to hear about college and what it was like to go to Washington D.C., and what we call the Mason-Dixon Line.

I had never been anywhere beyond my community. Our parents were very strict with us, and we honored our mother and father. We were taught to honor and obey our parents from the day we were born.

John was one of my favorite people when I was a child. There were a lot of times when we played hide-and-seek, giant-steps and ring-around-the-roses, and pockets-full-of-posies.

I did not make it out of grade school. I had rheumatic fever and became partially blind. Whenever John had the time, he would write and tell me that maybe someday, when he finished college and got a job, he would give my parents the money so I could see an eye specialist.

John didn't know, but a year after he went away to college, I became totally blind. I don't feel sorry for myself. My parents bought me a radio out of the year's crop money. There's a talk show hosted by a man named Arthur Godfrey, and I listen to him every day. One day he told a lady that she could be whatever she wanted to be. Believe it or not, I play the piano for our church.

It's getting late, and we are getting ready for bed. We have to go to the field tomorrow. I will wrap tobacco for half the day and then hurry home so my Aunt Sissie can finish my dress for Sunday to hear John's speech. I hope when he sees me, he won't feel sorry for me, for I can play any tune on the piano without looking at the keys.

Since I've been blind I've learned to do a lot. My cousins helped me in the church when they didn't have anything going on, and that's where I learned to play the piano. My gift to play the piano and make people happy comes from God—playing the music of God.

John went to college to become what he wanted to be.

Chapter Two

It's Sunday at last in our old farming town of Cedar Grove. My mother has been up since five o'clock in the morning. She made some of the best biscuits, sausage, ham, and white gravy—the best I ever tasted.

I can hear Ella Mae calling me. I tell her that I cannot come over early this morning. I have to help Mama finish the dinner we are preparing to take to church, and, boy, we really cooked all kinds of food. It looks as though it could feed two hundred people.

Anyway, I don't want to go over too early. John arrived late last night. He's probably up and, boy, I would not want him to see all these strings Mama put in my hair to make it straight. She wrapped my hair in a million strings. I know it will look nice once it's unwrapped, as style-wise, it's like Billie Holiday.

I like the way the stars fix their hair. Once I found a magazine in school. It had a lot of nice hairstyles in it, although mama would not allow me to look at the book because it had a boy kissing a girl on it. Mama and Daddy would really tear me to pieces if they found out about the book. Girls were taught that if you look at a boy, you would be in the family way, and boys were taught not to play with girls, because they will lead to trouble. Sometimes I wonder what the next generation will be like.

It's bath time now for everyone. Boy, am I tired of pumping water and boiling it on our wood stove so we can take a bath. I hate the lye soap that Mama makes. It makes me smell like gunpowder. I hate it, but we have to take a bath with something. I wish we could afford another wooden tub, because as soon as one of us finished, another wants to take a bath. There are eight of us and it takes around seven in the morning until about ten to get my younger sisters and brothers off to Sunday school.

We live behind the church, so we can see the cars as they pull up. I always like it when Sunday comes, for it's the only time and the only day I can meet a lot of people as they come to church. it is also a day no one has to go pick tobacco or do other field chores.

It's finally my turn now for a bath and my mother is boiling the water. She pours my water in the tub for me because I'm blind. She doesn't trust me to carry the bucket of hot water to the tub. She's afraid I might trip and fall and burn myself. It's the only thing I cannot, or am not, allowed to do for myself. As far as all the other chores around the house, there is never a problem. I was taught never to feel sorry for myself and never say you can't. That is why I feel so important to my family, my neighborhood, and my church, for God gives me the strength to go forward.

Sometimes life gets hard in our little community, but most of us don't feel sorry for ourselves. We go to school and harvest our crops. We don't look down upon ourselves as being poor or black. We look at ourselves as trying to be a part of our heritage, trying to get an education so that the next generation will have it a little better than we do. Our goal is: whoever gets an education always comes back to their roots and encourages others to do the same, and doesn't look back. Be a winner in whatever you do. That's why John Brower is back today, to share his dreams of being the first black anchorman in a big northern city.

It's time for me to go. I'm running late. Oh well, the music can't start in the church until I get there. I'm the only piano player in the community, so I must not keep them waiting.

Chapter Three

Cars, cars, cars everywhere. I'm glad we don't have a car and live a long distance away because it would be hard to find a parking space.

As I entered the church, the minister said to the congregation, with a big smile on his face, "Here's our piano player. Why, you're a couple of minutes late."

I was a little shy because other people came from a little town called Brown Summit to hear John speak. Some of the people came just to hear of Washington D.C., home of our great president.

My first selection came after the minister introduced John and spoke about what he had achieved. As I started playing *Amazing Grace* softly after the introduction; there were a number of ministers making speeches to the young people.

One speaker was Rev. Lomark, the minister from Brown Summit. He said in a touching speech, "From the moment you're conceived in your mother's womb, you are somebody. From the day you breathed your first breath, you are somebody. And never forget who you are, for you are God's creation and remember, all things are made possible by God."

It was a touching speech. Our older generation always quoted the Bible to us. It was a shield to take with you wherever you went.

They asked me to play another selection. It was John's favorite song when we were growing up. We sang this song while working in the field. It was called *What a Friend We Have in Jesus.* We sang many songs, but our favorite was *What a Friend We Have in Jesus.*

Our next speaker was Mrs. Virginia Steel, a 4-H Club worker for our school, and, boy, did she have a big announcement to make. She had wanted John to come home before she made her announcement. She started by saying that our neighborhood school would be closing and all children in grades one to twelve from Cedar Grove would attend school in Brown Summit, and we would have our first school bus.

Some of the children gasped as others' eyes dampened. Our school had been there since our mothers' time, but that was the new law of our state. The new school was larger and had more to offer.

There was another announcement about diphtheria shots and dental treatments that would be given to everyone. We had never had shots, and most of our people lived to be a ripe old age. The announcement took everyone by surprise.

When Mrs. Steel ended her surprise announcements, it was time for a solo sung by Antonette Gill. She had such a pretty voice. She sang, "In that great getting up morning, fare you well, fare you well. In that great getting up morning, fare you well, fare you well."

She had the church on its feet with her high notes. After her selection, it was time for our minister to speak.

He started by saying, "Today I'm proud to be the minister of Cedar Grove Methodist Church. And I'm also proud of one of ours. One young man who came home after graduating to be with us. It's hard to speak the words that are in my heart to you. Each and every one of you is a winner. You are winners because God had given you strength and knowledge to go forward, and you have put Him first in everything you've achieved. For without God, nothing is possible. You are the backbone of tomorrow's world. You are the product of our little country town. Go in the name of Jesus. Don't hate a person when he or she may not be your color. Don't hate a person if he or she knows more than you. Love your neighbors and your enemies as you would love yourself. As you climb the ladder, don't get so high, for you can fall. As you go to bigger cities, you will find a multitude of people in all colors, for people are like flowers and we must pick them equal. Brothers and sisters, as I leave you today, continue spreading God's word and love to your children so that their children will have God's love and kindness, a wonderful foundation to build on. May we have a selection by the choir? Let's all go by singing *The Old Rugged Cross.*"

The church was quiet after the hymn, and a warm feeling was in the air. We knew we were making our parents proud of us and that's all that mattered.

As John sat quietly and listened to our pastor speak those touching words of wisdom and determination, he looked happy to be home. He was to leave on Tuesday to return for an interview for his anchorman post.

John said his goodbyes to everyone and all wished him good luck. Our family never saw him leave because he left early, but I know he was happy going to the big city. I hoped he would be the first black ever to anchor the news. I was proud because he was from our little town. Some people call it a hick town, but I was proud to be a part of it. I knew John would say something about it, and that way it would give us all something to talk about.

Chapter Four

The next time I saw John's mother, she looked so sad. She had been hiding from us and she didn't look happy. Even John's sister seemed to avoid the community. She seemed unhappy also. Later on, we found out that John had been denied the anchorman post that he had worked so hard for. We heard that he took a cooking job in a big, fancy restaurant. We found out later that when he went for the interview, the people at WFAR didn't interview him. The story goes that they thought he was there for the night crew to clean up. He told them there must be a mistake. After he showed them all his paperwork, he was denied. People say he went into a depression.

He took a job near the local station as a waiter so he could see all the people who had denied him come in to eat. He was very quiet and, as time went by, he started to use heroin. He changed and changed fast.

He called an old college friend and told him of his disappointments. He asked him to get some poison that would kill quickly and silently. He was out to get revenge. He knew that two people who had denied and laughed at him had to die. He also knew they frequented the restaurant where he worked as a busboy, or did whatever other chores that needed to be done.

He stopped calling his family. He was out of control, with a wild look in his eyes. He never told people where he worked or what his problems were. When they asked him if everything was okay, he would just walk away.

One night his friend called and asked him why he wanted the poison. John told him that he was sending it to his mother, because she had a few wild dogs on her land and thought that they might have rabies.

The plot was developing. His friend had taken chemistry, so he knew how to kill anything quietly. John told him to mail it quickly before someone got bit because there was no money for rabies shots. The friend agreed. John was on his way to becoming a killer.

It was early December and John wanted to make sure he killed the two men before Christmas and, if possible, on Christmas Eve. He never gave a thought about the fact that they might have families, children, wives, or loved ones. He didn't care. All he thought of was how they had denied him the chance to become an anchorman.

I wished I could have been near him. I would have told him that being denied anything—work, play, or just playing a game of cards—is not the end of the world. He didn't understand that the men who had denied him were just doing their jobs. They had a superior. So what was he going to do—kill every one of them? Being an anchorman was even new to them, too. In our race, you have to crawl before you walk.

It was almost Christmas Eve. John waited patiently for his friend to send the poison. Everyone at work was beginning to talk about him, his many mood changes and hot temper. He began to drop things when he served people. Even the young ladies didn't interest him. He was out for revenge. He had completely given up. Everyone asked him if there was a problem, and thought that maybe they could help. He was too embarrassed to tell them he was a college graduate and had been turned down for an anchor post because of his race.

I wished he would have openly discussed his problems with someone. Maybe they would have told him that it wasn't the end of the world. Life goes on, and look at all the people who love you. They would have told him that he had come a long way to get this far. How many blacks could really go to college in the fifties? We were just happy being who we were. One seldom heard of killing in our town. If so, it was domestic and no one ever killed police officers. We had respect for all people, no matter who they were.

I knew John was very upset because he didn't get the job, but it didn't give him the right to take another human being's life.

Time was rapidly approaching and Christmas Eve was getting near. John had already chosen his victims. He was nervous, hoping his friend would get the poison he needed to start his killing spree.

John left work at 12:00 P.M., three days before Christmas Eve. He hoped that his friend had sent the poison. He didn't know that his next door neighbor had been holding the box for him. As soon as John returned upstairs, his neighbor heard his keys in the door and told him, "Hey man, I have a package for you. The mail was delivered early."

John knew it was time to start his killing spree. As he started wondering, he mind began to play tricks on him. He hoped that the two gentlemen, who normally ate at the restaurant every day, didn't go away for the holidays. He wanted to get the killing out of the way.

Chapter Five

He was on his mission as soon as possible. His family tried in vain to reach him by phone. They called his job, only to be told that he had left early. No one knew what was going on. John's mother wanted to come see her son, but she didn't have the money because it was Christmas and she had to buy her kids something. No, the only thing she could do was pray for him and hope he was okay.

The next morning, John got up early for work. He had injected some heroin into his arm the night before Christmas Eve and he was ready to kill. He probably knew that it would be the end, but he didn't care.

When he arrived for work, his co-workers asked him if he'd had a rough night. He didn't answer, but just stared into space. He put on his uniform and went out on the floor. People started to come in and give Christmas tips. John would not accept them; he didn't even thank them.

It was about noon when the two men came in from the television station who had denied him the job. They weren't happy because it was Christmas Eve, and they had to work.

John made sure that he took their orders. They didn't know that John was the young black man they had turned down for the anchorman post. He was just another busboy in their book. One of the men asked John to take a Christmas gift, but again he refused.

When their order was called, John slipped the poison from his pocket and emptied the bottle on the plates. It was enough to kill an army of people. The poison was odorless and tasteless. They would be dead in a second.

As he gave them their plates, he said, "Merry Christmas."

One of the men said, "Oh, I see you smile after all."

John disappeared from the restaurant as quickly as possible. The two men ate their soup first. When they started on their dinner, their deaths came quickly. The owner of the restaurant thought it was food poisoning, but he noticed that no one else had gotten sick.

As their bodies were being removed, the news was already spreading all over.

John rushed home. He knew that he would be caught soon. He wrote his parents a farewell letter, and he also wrote one to me. It read:

> My dear niece,
> I never really told you that I loved you when we were growing up. I think you know that I've done something real bad now and I have to pay for my crimes. Don't cry at my funeral. Just play *Pass Me Not, Oh Gentle Savior, Hear My Humble Cry.*

I was so sorry for the people John had killed. I thought about their families, children, and wives, and that they wouldn't be home for Christmas. I prayed for the families. Sometimes I wonder why man kills and why people hate.

It was about three o'clock in the morning when a lady on the third floor heard something. She said that it sounded like something had fallen out of the window. It was John. He had fallen to his death. His body was picked up about six o'clock in the morning. He had committed suicide. He had left instructs about who to notify.

When the news reached our little community, everyone was shocked. No one knew why an educated man of John's standard would do such a thing. Maybe someday they would find out the whole truth, but it wasn't time to ask questions.

It was a long ordeal John's family had to bear. First, they had to get him home, and I asked everyone to help with the expenses.

As the day drew near, you could hear John's family crying. It was very sad. Maybe someday another young person would rise up from the ashes and would go on to succeed. I felt sorry for everyone involved in the senseless murders and suicide.

Two days passed, and we finally got the money to bring John's body home. He was to be buried in Cedar Grove Cemetery. His preacher when he was a little boy was to do the eulogy.

John's body was finally home. His funeral was set to be held on Sunday, a week after Christmas. People prepared food for the wake. We had plenty of food because we canned our food during the summer months, so it wasn't a problem on our part to help out. Other people made dresses to help out John's big family. Some of our white folks brought all kinds of meats. It was hog killing time and they brought meats and Christmas toys for our children. They did this every year. They had been very kind to us. Some would attend John's funeral.

I was suppose to play the piano and give a speech. It went like this: "Today we have come together to bury one of our own. The kindness of God never ceases. John's dreams and memories have come to an end. We will miss him dearly. We will teach our children to love more closely, never to hate. If the things you strive for don't come your way when you want them to, God does not give you the right to take another man's life. So we celebrate the memories of John. Not for what he did, but we hope God will find a place for him in heaven. I'm sorry to say, but this is the end of a new beginning."

I hope you've enjoyed reading THE ANCHORMAN MURDERS as much as I've enjoyed telling my story.

Thank you,
Ethel Headen

Part II

The Next Generation from Cedar Grove

Chapter One

It's in the 70's now, a long way from the late 50's. I think about my ancestors a lot. Some of them died long ago. I miss my old nanny May and the rest of the older set. I'm a grandma now. I will never forget my Uncle John Brower. To this day his name is still fresh in our minds. I'm sorry he didn't get the chances we have today. I live in a northern city now where I met a very nice man. His name is Bill. We have five kids, some of whom are in college.

Yes, I'm still visually handicapped, but I've learned to deal with my blindness. My husband works for a correctional institution. It's a very dangerous job, but someone has to do it. I've gotten scholarships for two of my kids. Kids are not the same any more. You have grandmothers at the age of 38 and a lot of them are doped up. How can they tell their children anything when they are nothing themselves?

I'm very proud of my children. They don't drink or smoke. I taught them to put God first and then everything will fall into place.

When I left the South in the late 50's, it was a sad ordeal. I went to the gravesite to say my good-byes to my mother and father and also to my Uncle John.

I took the Greyhound bus. At that time they used to have a big greyhound dog on the side of the bus. I was happy to leave. My cousin, Mary, had written me and asked me to come and go to the doctors up north for my eyesight. I was excited because I thought they could cure my eyesight, but it was too late. They eye condition had been with me since I was nine years old. The fever I'd had when growing up in the South had taken its toll.

Mary took me to a place called Relief Fund to get me a check for living expenses. We sat there all day. Finally they put me on. I don't know how much she was paid. I didn't ask her because I was glad just to stay with her. I was seventeen years old when I arrived at my aunt's home. I wasn't about to live on a relief check. I didn't like handouts, so I called the Handicapped for the Blind. I will never forget how they called me in for an evaluation and they told me they would teach me how to make brooms and other things.

Oh, boy, things started to look up for me. I went on a Tuesday and was told to report for work on the following Monday. I was so happy to get a job, since nothing beats working. Now Mary didn't have to worry about getting home relief checks for me. I was young and I was working. I didn't let my eyesight stand in my way.

Chapter Two

Things were really starting to look up. I was doing something I really liked and getting paid for it. The many other blind people who worked with me taught me the skills they had learned.

I received a few paychecks and was ready to move from my cousin's house. The blind association got me a one-bedroom place not far from my workplace. They were looking to get me a dog. I was really blessed.

I'd always been independent, even when growing up in the South. I played the piano for the church for a few dollars a month, enough to buy a pair of shoes or something for my parents. They had so many donations. I asked if I had to pay for this or that, and they said the Blind Association gave help to people who were blind. I was so thrilled and thankful. I'd never had that kind of help before.

We worked very hard in the fields where I came from. We raised tobacco and corn. Corn was our main source of income. I was so happy to be away from farming and happy to be making my own living. Here in the big city I might go back to school and become a sign language teacher. I wanted to be something before I died, and to know my life was not in vain. The next thing I planned to do was go to a church, any church, for all are God's place of worship. For all these things to happen so quickly for me had to be an act of God.

I heard the government was giving grants for poor children to go to school. Many of my distant cousins had already signed up for college.

They were not farming any more. I didn't know who was working our fields this year since most of our children were going to school. I knew I would never go back to the farm, although ever as a blind person I knew how to wrap tobacco and shuck corn.

Chapter Three

It was the end of summer and I was enjoying my apartment and my new job. I was going with a couple of my friends to a dance at a place called Savoy Manor. I hadn't been anywhere except work and home tidying up my apartment. "All work and no play makes life dull today," was an old slogan my grandmother used.

I waited for my friends to pick me up, some of whom weren't blind, but only visually handicapped. We were going shopping for clothes. I was getting a pretty red dress. I thought red was a beautiful color to attract a man (smile). I wasn't look for a man, but if one came along and would take me as I was, who knew what life had in store?

My friends arrived and we went shopping. It would be the night of all nights.

Shopping was fun. My friends, June, Carol, and Joan, kept teasing me. "Oh, girl, you are going to meet your husband tonight."

I was very nervous. I was a country girl in the big city going to a dance. I was in shock. It was time to get dressed. I thought about the times I had to boil water on the stove to take a bath in a wooden tub. Everything was so modern; all I had to do was turn on the tub and hot and cold water came out. I couldn't believe my eyes.

Well, my friends arrived and we were ready to go. People in the street told us how good we looked, especially the young men.

Chapter Four

We arrived at the club around ten o'clock and it was packed. They had a naked girl doing a strip tease. My friends filled me in on everything. They weren't visually handicapped the way I was. A couple of guys came over to our table and asked for a dance. At the time, we weren't interested because there was too much going on.

My girlfriend started to tease me about one guy in particular. She said, "He was staring at you and I be he will come back to our table."

Sure enough, he came back and asked me if I would dance with him. I froze in my seat. I had on dark sunglasses and I didn't want him to know I was visually handicapped. Anyway, I said, "Later. Have a seat."

As we sat in our lounge chairs, he asked for my name. I told him that it was Ella Mae. He said, "I like Ella, leave the Mae off."

He smiled. I was very shy because I didn't want him to stare at my eyes. Anyway, after a while he didn't say anything about my sunglasses. He asked for a date. Even though I couldn't see him, he had a very nice northern voice. I kept telling him that I didn't feel up to dancing. Soon I knew I had to tell him about my eyesight. He excused himself from my table, so he could go tell his friends where we were sitting.

He waited a long time before telling me his name. I thought that maybe he was married and didn't want to tell me. Anyway, he finally did. He said, "My name is Bill, and I'm not married and not engaged to anyone. I'm also in the Navy. I'm stationed at Quonset Point, Rhode Island. I'm on liberty and decided to hang out with my friends."

He called to his friends to sit at our table. My friends were already dancing with other guys on the dance floor, but when all of the Navy guys came over, they dropped the men they were dancing with.

Just from the sound of Bill's voice, I fell in love. He had a northern accent and I had a southern accent. He was very kind. I asked him about his parents. His mother was living, but his father had died. He also came from a large family. We had a lot in common, besides being from large families.

The night was coming to a close and we were about to leave. Bill asked if he and his friends could escort us home. It was late and we were all girls. Anything could happen.

Chapter Five

I'd had a wonderful time at the dance. On Sunday, I was looking for Bill. I had told him about my eyesight. He didn't seem to care because I could do anything and go any place that a person with normal vision could.

There was a knock on the door and it was Bill. He even brought his own breakfast. I only had a room and there was no cooking. We listened to some old songs on the radio. He basically told me about his childhood and I told him about mine.

As time went by, Bill came to my house every time he had liberty. He told me that he was in love with me. I said to him, "You only met me a few weeks ago."

But he said, "You know when true love strikes and I don't want to strike out."

Bill didn't know it, but I'd really fallen for him that first night at the dance. I never told him that, though.

He said he had less than a year to serve at Quonset Point. He said he might go back to school and take up aviation mechanics. It was a new time and a new era and people of color could go to school and become what they wanted to, even with help from the government. Bill said he would use his GI Bill. I didn't know what a GI Bill was.

My ancestors had gone into service in World War II. I think all of them were potato peelers. I was too young to know. I will never forget my Uncle John Brower and the anchorman murders. I wish he was here today to see all the progress people of color have made.

Bill was about to leave. He had a ride back to the base. I looked forward to seeing him the following week if he could get liberty.

The week passed quickly and to my surprise there was a knock at the door. It was Bill. He gave me a little kiss and hug. He said, "Hurry, we are going to a candlelight dinner and afterwards we will go and meet my mom and brothers and sisters."

I was really in shock. I couldn't imagine that a poor blind Southern girl like myself had moved up so quickly.

After our dinner, we were on our way to meet his folks. He knocked on the door and called for his mother to put her dog away because it bit strangers. When the dog had been put away, they said, "Come in."

No one said anything about my eyesight. Bill must have talked to his people before.

It was nearly Thanksgiving before I saw them again. They were very nice. They had a lot of food, but I was too full to eat. They invited me back for Thanksgiving. They even had relatives in the South, not too far from where I was from. When I talked about Cedar Grove Township, they remember John Brower and the anchorman murders. I didn't dare tell them that person was my uncle. They said things had changed since the anchorman murders.

The North had all kinds of schools. Bill hurried to change the subject as his people were getting deep into talking about education and I didn't have much education. I was from the South, the farm. All I knew how to do was to play piano.

I had already signed up for blind school in the fall. If I went long enough, I could even go to college. I would work a half-day job and go to school the other half. It was something I wanted to do because I couldn't go to school in the South. They had no visually handicapped schools where I lived.

So you see, I was going to explore everything. I'd learned never to live on self-pity, but always to look ahead and explore different things. We are not living in a world of self-pity, but in a world where you can get an education and get paid for going to school at the same time. My people in the South could not believe all the progress I made. Self-determination was the key to my success.

It was fall and getting really chilly. I'd have to buy a new fall coat. My coworker told me that it was very cold here in winter. I couldn't ask for more. I had a new job and a nice sailor in my life. I was on cloud nine. God wanted me to find happiness and He blessed me to do just that.

There's an old saying: "What you were taught as a child will follow you all the days of your life." If you ad the old teaching. You could still hear them talking. I didn't know what my parents were talking about at the time, but everything they taught me crossed my path.

Chapter Six

Oh, Thanksgiving was next Thursday. I wished I could cook Bill a dinner. Maybe he thought that because I was blind, I couldn't cook. I wished I could cook him a southern-style turkey and sweet potatoes with all the trimming, but I had no stove, just a room. I hoped the next year to get a studio apartment where I could at least have a stove.

I'd been to Bill's house a couple of times. They gave me ready-cooked food to take home. My girlfriend lived around the corner so she took me there. I hoped I wasn't wearing out my welcome. They were so nice to me. Bill's younger brothers were in high school and they enjoyed taking me back home.

Well, we were two days from Thanksgiving. I'd been dating Bill for ten months and it seemed like only yesterday when we met. He said that he couldn't wait to go home for the holidays because he had two surprises for me. I thought I knew one surprise. He was getting me a television and the other surprise I didn't know.

His brothers almost told me about the phone. They were joking around and they asked each other who would wait on the phone Monday at my room. When I asked, "Who's getting a phone?" they became very quiet.

I had a lot to do. For one thing I might go home for Christmas. It was my birthday Christmas Eve. I hadn't been back to Cedar Grove since I left. I would spend Thanksgiving with Bill and his family and Christmas with mine in the South.

Tomorrow was Thanksgiving and my friend Emily would be over soon. She was going with me to buy something nice that would catch Bill's eye. She picked out pretty clothes to attract people. Everyone always told her that she looked nice.

I had to hurry back. Bill said that he was coming to take me out.

A knock finally came at my door. It was Bill. I was so happy that he had made it home. Now I knew I would have fun on Thanksgiving. He had a small bottle of wine called Thunderbird. Most of the sailors were drinking Thunderbird wine. It was cheap, and, after all, the service wasn't paying a great deal of money.

As we sat down at my table, he said, "Close your eyes. Give me your hand." He took my ring finger and put a big diamond engagement ring on it. I was so excited. He got down on his knees, still holding my hand, and asked me to marry him. I was crying, happy, all smiles and felt like I had butterflies in my stomach. Boy, coming to a big city really had changed my luck, and with God all things are possible.

Well, it was Thanksgiving, and I would wear my beautiful diamond engagement ring to Bill's family's house for dinner. I was still in shock. It seemed as if we were moving too fast. He said he wanted a wedding date before he went back to the base. I thought of Easter time. It would be spring and all of the flowers would be in bloom. I would tell him my thoughts later.

It was time to go. Bill was ringing my bell. We had a code. He rang two short rings and I knew it was him. We were about to arrive at his mother's house. We could smell the food as we walked up the stairs.

"Come on in, rest your coat."

The first to stare at my finger was Bill's sister, Annie. "Oh, that's the ring my brother has been telling us about. So when is the big day?"

I stood nervously and said, "Easter of next year."

Bill said, "Yes, yes, yes." I had not told him a date.

As we were eating, Bill's brother said, "Look, it's snowing." We were getting our first sample of winter.

Bill's mother, Abby, said, "I don't want to rush you all, but get Ella home before the storm. The radio says six inches of snow."

We finished dinner and were on our way back home. Bill took me back to my room. He had to hurry back to his mother's house, for the blizzard had come in. he later called his friends and told them that he couldn't make it back to base if it kept snowing the way it was. Anyway, I was glad to have Bill around because I couldn't see to go out in the snow. Everything was working out for me.

Chapter Seven

Bill had less than a year before his discharge from the Navy. He was counting the days. We were going to be married at Easter and we decided to have the ceremony on the base. We didn't have money to have a church wedding. Anyway, everything was free, including all the food you wanted to eat.

My mother could not attend. She was very sick with stomach cancer. We had to sell our farm for her medical care and now she received Social Security. My father dies years ago from heart disease. We really loved that farm, but to tell the truth, there was no one to farm it anymore. Their descendants didn't have to farm because they were all going to school to become schoolteachers, nurses, and some were even studying to be doctors.

Spring was just around the corner. We had a very bad winter with a lot of snow and ice. I was getting ready to be married. It was just a few weeks away. I wasn't going to wear a gown, but just a simple dress. Bill's brother would be the only one from the family attending. We'd have a dinner when we returned. His Navy buddies would be our family, since ours were too poor to attend.

The last time Bill came home, he brought me a little record player and a couple of records. The one I liked was the song, *When We Get Married, We'll Have a Big Celebration*. I played it day and night when I came home from work. The only thing was, I wasn't having a big celebration.

Chapter Eight

It was hard to believe it was only two weeks before my wedding day. Time was getting near. I picked up my dress. I was going to wear a two-piece white suite. White is for when a woman is pure. I still had my innocence. I'd never been with a man before. That was why Bill was so nice to me. A man likes to feel that he's the first one. We never talked about sex on the farm. People were mum and didn't tell us things. I was taught that if you looked at a boy, you could have children, so a lot of our young girls had children out of wedlock. In the South, mothers would keep their children away from you if you had a baby out of wedlock.

Anyway, it was getting late and I had to work the next day.

When I went to work, all the girls were feeling my ring and saying how beautiful it felt. Because we were blind, we used our senses of touch and smell. God gave us an inner mind. We were very gifted people. The girls were getting together for a little bridal party at our job. They kept telling me, "Next week you will be Mrs. Bill Brown."

I had butterflies in my stomach. I had packed my bags, waiting like any other bride-to-be for the big day.

Today was Friday. Bill would be home. I couldn't wait to him the things I had bought. He couldn't see my wedding dress because they say it's bad luck. I didn't need bad luck. I'd been having such good luck. It seemed like I was dreaming and could not wake up.

Bill came home right on time. He said everything was set for the wedding next Sunday. He got the chaplain at the base to marry us. We would have a little ceremony there. He wanted his brother to be there and his best friend, Frank, so I let him decide whom he chose to be the best man.

Today was my last day of work. The girls had a party at lunchtime and gave me a lot of gifts. I was very happy.

When Bill came over, I'd show him the gifts. I hoped I had enough room since my place was so little. But I'd make room. All the gifts were precious to me, especially since they were all given from the heart. They gave me a linen towel set, and even a knife set. The cab driver helped me with all the packages. He was very nice. Right away he picked up my Southern accent.

Bill came over a few minutes after I got home. He was every excited about the gifts. He also had good news. His friend, Frank, who had a car, would take us to get married on Sunday. He was also stationed with Bill. A lot of sailors got a ride with Frank when they were coming home.

I missed my mother. She was too sick to come, but I knew her prayers were with me. I hoped that the good Lord would take her soon. She was suffering from cancer of the stomach and was in constant pain. I knew she was there in my heart and I couldn't ask for more.

Bill was getting ready to leave. He smiled and said, "Tomorrow you will be Mrs. Ella Brown."

It sounded nice to be called Mrs. Brown. I told him, "Be careful going home."

He said, "It's early. I've been used to going to bed real early. The people here don't go to a party before ten at night."

Chapter Nine

Our big day arrived. We were on the Navy base. All the sailors were lined up.

Frank and Bill's brother said, "Oh, this is beautiful."

Frank teased us by saying, "Sometimes little weddings are better than big ones." (Smile)

I had ten minutes to change my dress. I was getting nervous and my heart was pumping. In my mind, this was it—for better or worse, 'til death do us part.

As the Navy band played Bill's favorite song, I began to walk down the aisle. The song was *Because You Came To Me.* I wished the whole world could have been there. It was just beautiful. The Navy really had everything decked out. I walked with my brother-in-law Robert. His knees were shaking and so were mine. I liked the song *Because You Came to Me.*

After we took our wedding vows, the band played *Ave Maria.* It was beautiful. Bill gave me a big kiss. The Navy had the mess hall all decorated. No one even noticed that I was blind.

I really thought about my parents that day. Also my Uncle John Brower, who came to a northern city to be an anchorman and was denied equal rights for a job. Anyway, everything was working out for me. The Navy gave Bill a check for $500.00. We could get an apartment with it. No one knew how happy Bill made me. As for a honeymoon, we couldn't afford one. We would use our time to look for a larger place.

Frank brought us back to the city. I was a little drunk with all the champagne and wine toasting.

As we approached our room, the door was ajar. A burglar had robbed me of all the wedding gifts that my co-workers had given me. It is a hurting feeling when you have very little and someone takes what little you do have.

Bill said, "That's it. We will look for an apartment tomorrow. That's okay, we have plenty of love for each other. Whoever took this will not prosper."

The next day after a night of whirlwind lovemaking we were out looking for an apartment. We found a two-bedroom, very nice, and not too far from Bill's mother's. We paid one month security and one month rent and moved in the same day. We bought a little high-riser to sleep on.

I was glad that the Armed Forces gave Bill a thirty-day leave. I was going t miss him when he went back. I had two weeks off and we were going to live it to the fullest. Who cared? We were in love.

Chapter Ten

As I told you in the beginning, from this marriage to Bill Brown, we had five children; two are in college and the rest in grade school. My mother dies of cancer shortly after we were married. Bill's mother also dies from heart disease and most of his family moved away.

Bill got out of the Navy with an honorable discharge. He also landed a job with the Correction Department. He's still a good husband and father. I'm going to an eye specialist. Hopefully one day I will be able to see. Bill has good insurance, so I'm undergoing a lot of tests. That will be my second goal in life: to see my children and maybe grandchildren one day.

This is the end but also a new beginning for at least one of John Brower's relatives from Cedar Grove.